# The Perfect Guest

## Paula Metcalf

**WALKER BOOKS**
AND SUBSIDIARIES
LONDON · BOSTON · SYDNEY · AUCKLAND

For my nephews and niece ~
Ruben, Jody, George, Jacob, Caspar,
and Harriet

Walter was very proud of his beautiful home.
He loved his pretty ornaments,
his polka-dotty tablecloth
and his glorious garden.

Above all else, he loved his sparkly new teapot —
just thinking about it made him smile!

One morning, Walter's friend
Pansy called…

"I haven't seen you for ages!
Shall I come and visit?"

"Oh, yes! That would
be delightful!"

Walter couldn't wait to see his teeny-weeny squirrel friend!
First, he needed to smarten himself up ...

and make everything absolutely perfect for her stay!
There were still more jobs to be done when...

DING
DONG!

# Pansy was early!

Walter was very happy to see her ... but he wasn't ready!
He hadn't even finished mending his trousers!

"Let's catch up over a cup of tea," giggled Pansy,
"then I'll help you. I'm really good at sewing!"

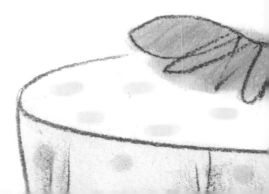

The mention of "tea" was music to Walter's ears —
he couldn't wait to show off his new teapot.

"It's gorgeous!" gasped Pansy.

"Why, thank you!"
grinned Walter.

How wonderful
it was to have
a guest!

After their tea, they set to work.

Walter carefully
ironed his socks ...

Pansy baked her
special lemon cake ...

and then
she got sewing!

"Finished!" Pansy announced proudly.
"There were loads of holes by the way,
   including two REALLY big ones
   at the bottom."

Walter took a closer look.
"Oh!" he gulped. "Oh, dear! Those were actually *legholes*!"
"Oops," replied Pansy.

Pansy wanted to make up for her mistake and soon found a way...

*Doo-bee-doo,*
*measuring and making...*

She made something
very special just
for Walter.

*Ta-da!*

"These are splendid,"
said Walter,
dancing about in his
new trousers.
"And the fabric is exactly
what *I* would
have chosen!"

*Hooray!*

It was a new day and Walter was eager to show off his new trousers. He did a little stretch and looked out at the glorious sunshine through the trouser-shaped hole in his curtains...

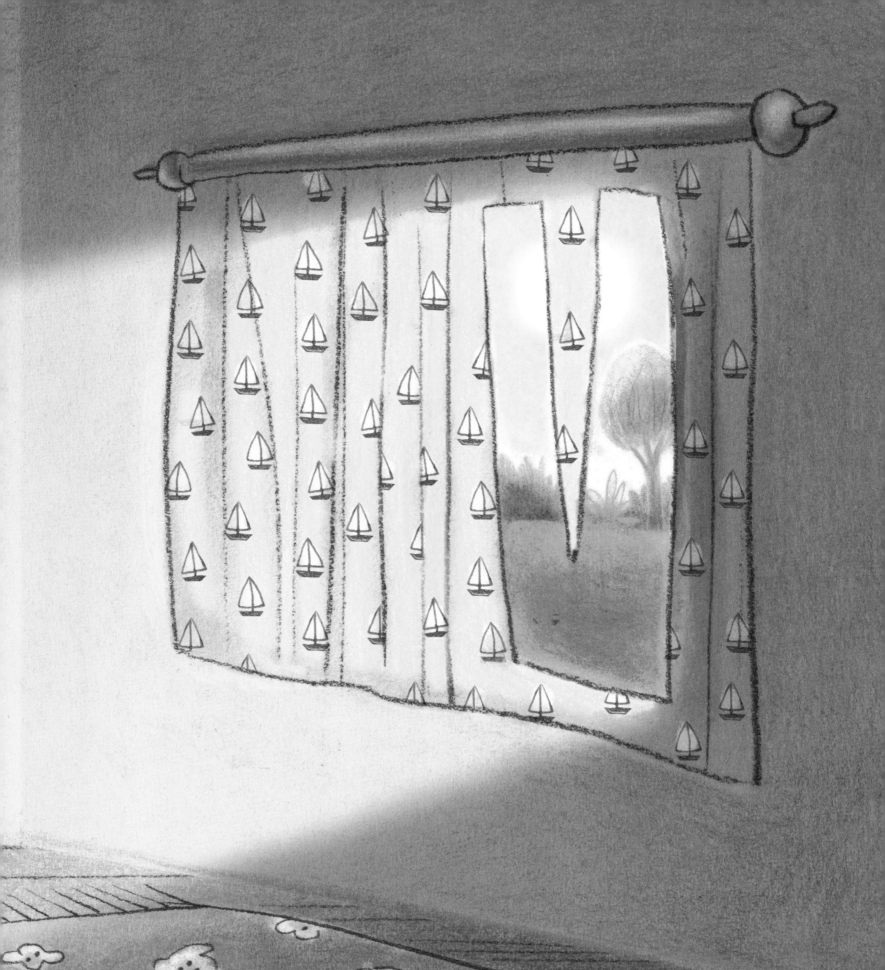

Trouser-shaped

HOLE

in his

CURTAINS?!

At times like this, only one thing could help.
"I need chocolate," muttered Walter. But when he opened
the box … his face dropped. "I don't understand!" he said.
"These were brand NEW!"

Pansy began to feel a little hot around the whiskers.
"Erm … maybe it's one of those boxes that comes with
free holders?" she suggested. "You know, to keep
spare chocolates in?"

"We'll have to have cake instead," sighed Walter.
"Would you like some, Pansy?"
"Yes please!" she replied and took a slice.

When they'd finished eating, Pansy got the vacuum cleaner out to suck up the crumbs.

*Yikes!*

But it was rather powerful for such a little squirrel.

*Double-yikes!*

# "Phew!
## At least my precious teapot is safe!"

Next, Pansy set about
the washing up.

*La, la, la! I love washing!*

*H-e-e-eave!*

*Oh-oh-oh...*

"I'm so sorry," sniffed Pansy. "Let me glue your teapot back together," she offered.

Walter shook his head.

"Well, what else can I help with?" she asked. "Em ... maybe some dusting?"

Walter thought about his precious ornaments ... it made him feel very nervous. Then he had an idea. "You could pop outside and water my carrots for me?"

Time to make everything perfect again!

Walter spent all afternoon mending, cleaning ...

dusting and sweeping. *Almost* spotless!

"Ooh! It must be time to check on Pansy," thought Walter.

"Em … I've had a little accident," said Pansy. "Please could you, um, bring the mop?"

Walter couldn't believe his eyes! He rushed back inside. But when he came out, he wasn't carrying a mop…

Pansy frowned. "How on earth are we going to fix things with those?" she asked.

"I've ALWAYS wanted a sailing boat!"
said Walter.
"Thank you so much Pansy,
you're the most
PERFECT GUEST ...

and my
very best
FRIEND!"